SIXTEEN
STRING JACK
and the Garden of Adventure

~ TOM POW ~

Illustrated by IAN ANDREW

For Margaret, Mia,
Ed and Emma
(IA)

For the children of Rosemount Street,
and in memory of Hannah Moffat
(TP)

Daisy stands beside her grandmother in an overgrown garden. Behind the trees and the bushes and the long grass, Granny knows there is a river. But she cannot see it.

It makes her sad to see the garden this way. And it makes her sad to see the house with its window frames rotting, its slates missing and its walls beginning to crack.

It is as if the house has not been able to bear seeing its garden forgotten.

'It wasn't always like this, Daisy,' says Granny. 'Not in Grandmother Maggie's time.'

Daisy's granny remembers the stories *her* grandmother told of when she had worked in the Big House. Then it had been a very fine house indeed. Grandmother Maggie had been a young woman then – still a girl, really – and, as she had told the stories, part of her seemed to become Young Maggie again.

'What are you thinking about, Granny?' asks Daisy.

'Oh, I'm just remembering. Remembering the stories that my grandmother told me about this place. I think you would have had fun in the garden back then.'

The stories Grandmother Maggie told concerned two brothers who lived in the house and a boy who arrived at their school one day. The brothers were Stewart and Hal, and the new boy was called Jamie. Almost immediately, the three of them became firm friends.

'My name is Dare Devil Dick,' announced Stewart to Jamie. 'And I'm going to call you Sixteen String Jack.'

'Sixteen String Jack! I like the sound of that,' said Jamie. 'It's a powerful name.'

'Yes, it is, my *bucko*,' said Dare Devil Dick. 'It's the name of a fearless rascal.' Then, more quietly, he told Sixteen String Jack, 'By the way, my brother, Hal, knows everybody in this town with a peg-leg. Retired pirates, that's what they are.'

'The only retired pirates are *dead* pirates,' said Sixteen String Jack. 'They must be ghosts!'

Dare Devil Dick liked the sound of that.

Jamie was small for his age, but he had bright brown eyes and heaps of energy. There were lots of things he liked to do. He liked fishing and he liked cricket. He also enjoyed dressing up and taking part in plays. Sometimes, Jamie asked Maggie how he looked in a new costume.

'I've got far too much to do to be thinking about things like that,' said Maggie. 'If I don't get these vegetables ready for dinner . . . Well, I don't know, I sometimes think a girl is worth twenty of you boys.'

But, as she was saying it, Jamie could tell that, inside, she was smiling.

The greatest adventures the boys had took place in the garden of the Big House.

Honour was at stake when pirate took on pirate. *Pirate's honour*, of course. The enemy tried to drive the boys down towards the crocodile-infested river. They fought back fearlessly.

But look! – Dare Devil Dick has tripped on a tree root; his sword has gone flying through the air. The pirates and the Indians – where did that lot come from? – are rushing towards him, armed to the teeth! The game is surely up for Dare Devil Dick.

But, wait! Sixteen String Jack has seen the danger he is in and turns to face the enemy. He is *hopelessly* outnumbered, but still – can you believe it? – he is laughing. He catches the flying sword . . .

. . . and he throws it back to Dare Devil Dick. 'Oh yes, *me hearties,*'
he shouts in their faces, 'you didn't know what you were doing when
you took on Sixteen String Jack! And Dare Devil Dick!'

Many times on the high seas, on a Saturday afternoon, their pirate crew was wrecked on a desert island and they were forced to live in a cave. They threw stones up into the trees to bring down coconuts. They lit fires by rubbing two sticks together.

On long summer nights, after tea, other school friends would join them and they would play till the lamps were lit and they were called into the house. Maggie liked this time of the year best. When it grew dark, light shone from the open windows over the garden. There was something magical about it then.

Jamie sat with Stewart and Hal on steps that led out to the garden. Jamie narrowed his eyes and peered into the shadows. Sometimes, he thought he glimpsed something moving there – maybe a bird, maybe a branch waving in the breeze.

Or maybe the outline of a boy – the shadow of a boy who could carry on the adventure while he slept back in his own bed.

Mr Gordon, Stewart and Hal's father, spent his days as a lawyer, surrounded by piles of paperwork. When he could, he liked to watch the boys play at the end of his serious day. But his was a very demanding job, and often he had to spend many hours in his study. He was never to be disturbed there, so Mrs Gordon would ask the boys how they had been passing their time. Maggie liked to be around then, for what a tale Jamie could spin!

At times, Jamie enjoyed playing with his friends so much that he thought to himself, 'Wouldn't it be wonderful to have adventures like this all the time? Wouldn't it be wonderful never to grow up and to become serious like Mr Gordon has to be?'

In fact, Jamie liked making up stories more than anything. He began to write them down. He put them into books and into plays. Eventually, he became the most famous writer in Britain, and the most highly paid.

After many years, Jamie returned to the town where he had gone to school. There is a photograph of him surrounded by pupils dressed as fairies. He never grew much taller, so the fairies are not much smaller than he is.

He gave a talk that day. He said being a boy in the town had been a very happy time for him. And he said that it was playing in the Gordons' garden that, in time, gave us Peter Pan.

'*Peter Pan*, Daisy,' says Granny. 'Think of all the children who have heard of him and of the adventures he has had.'

Daisy and her grandmother stand in the overgrown garden, as the shadows lengthen in the late afternoon. Daisy thinks she sees, between branches, something shining in the river. Is it a tiny wave – or is it the gleaming tooth of a crocodile? She is seeing things through Grandmother Maggie's eyes, and through the eyes of the small boy who told stories of the games he played.

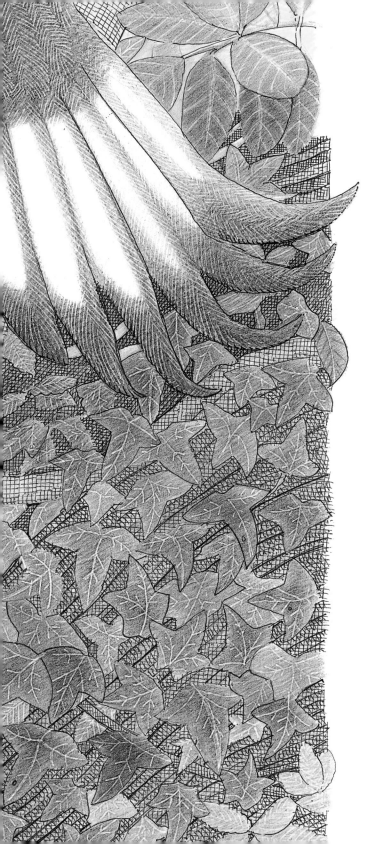

Deep in the shadows, she sees a movement. Is it the flutter of a bird? Or simply the movement of a branch. Then she hears a piercing cry.

Coo-ca-roo-coo!
Coo-ca-roo-coo!

Granny smiles. 'Did you hear that, Daisy?' she asks. 'Did you hear that?'

Peter Pan is back and the garden will come alive again.

Most of this story is true. In fact, the only part that's not true is this: although the Gordon family had a kitchen maid, we can't be sure that her name was Maggie – or that she had a grand-daughter. The Gordons' house was and is called Moat Brae, a Georgian mansion standing next to Dumfries Academy, though it is a long time since the Gordon family lived there. Stewart and Hal *were* the two great friends with whom J.M. Barrie (1860–1937) played – played the kinds of games described in this story. You may also like to know that Sixteen String Jack was a real person – a famous eighteenth-century highway-man. He liked dressing up too, and wore eight coloured strings tied below each knee.

J.M. Barrie did return to Dumfries Academy, as a very rich and famous writer. On this visit, on which he was awarded the Freedom of Dumfries (11 December 1924), he spoke of his school life: 'I think the five years or so that I spent there were probably the happiest of my life.'

Recalling his time playing in the garden of Moat Brae house, he commented, '. . . when the shades of night began to fall, certain young mathematicians shed their triangles, and became pirates in a sort of odyssey that was long afterwards to become the play of Peter Pan. For our escapades in a certain Dumfries garden, which is enchanted land to me, were certainly the genesis of that nefarious work.'

For many years, the house lay empty and the garden overgrown. But, in 2009, the Peter Pan Moat Brae Trust took over both the garden and the house and it is in the process of restoring the historic garden and the house itself. The vision of the trust is to turn the house into a National Centre for Children's Literature and Story-telling – thus honouring J.M. Barrie's imagination and the role that Moat Brae had in shaping it.

Tom and Ian would like to thank the Peter Pan Moat Brae Trust, Dumfries Museum and Graham Gordon, grandson of Henry (Hal) Gordon, for their help in the making of this book.

First published in 2015 by
Birlinn Limited
West Newington House
10 Newington Road
Edinburgh
EH9 1QS

www.birlinn.co.uk

Text copyright © Tom Pow 2015
Illustrations copyright © Ian Andrew 2015

The moral right of Tom Pow to be identified
as the author of this work has been asserted
by him in accordance with the Copyright,
Designs and Patents Act 1988

All rights reserved. No part of this publication
may be reproduced, stored or transmitted
in any form without the express written
permission of the publisher.

ISBN: 978 1 78027 226 9

British Library Cataloguing-in-Publication Data
A catalogue record for this book is available
from the British Library

Designed and typeset by Mark Blackadder

The publisher acknowledges investment from

ALBA | CHRUTHACHAIL

towards the publication of this volume

PETER PAN
MOAT BRAE
TRUST

Printed and bound in Latvia by Livonia

RIVER
NITH

Moat

53

MOAT BRAE

Posts

57

Posts